# THE STORY OF STORIES

# THE STORY OF STORIES

Enjoy the
Story !
Dare to touch the
pages !

Vincent E. Pilkington-Landreville

*Landreville*

**To order additional copies of this book, contact:**
Xlibris Corporation
1-888-795-4274
www.Xlibris.com
Orders@Xlibris.com
46384

# CONTENTS

Acknowledgements ..................................................................... 7

Chapter 1: The Mysterious Book ................................................. 9

Chapter 2: A New World .......................................................... 13

Chapter 3: Friends ................................................................... 20

Chapter 4: The Brownie Colony ................................................ 24

Chapter 5: The Giant .............................................................. 29

Chapter 6: Rejoice ................................................................... 32

Chapter 7: The Wrong Portal! .................................................. 34

Chapter 8: The Story ............................................................... 39

Chapter 9: The Dungeons ........................................................ 44

Chapter 10: The Pool of Water ................................................ 49

Chapter 11: The Dark Staircase ................................................ 56

Chapter 12: Out of the Darkness .............................................. 60

Chapter 13: The Pynazims ....................................................... 65

Chapter 14: Into the Pynazim .................................................. 69

Chapter 15: Down the Hallway ................................................ 75

Chapter 16: Marcelieuse Fonleiy .............................................. 80

Chapter 17: The Fight .............................................................. 84

Chapter 18: Back Home Once Again ........................................ 88

Chapter 19: The Manombo Forest ............................................ 91

Chapter 20: Carnivores! ........................................................... 94

Chapter 21: The Hut ............................................................... 100

Chapter 22: The Meeting ......................................................... 104

# ACKNOWLEDGEMENTS

First and foremost, I would like to thank my two wonderful illustrators, James Peters and Emma Awe. The work you have done is greatly appreciated.

To my family, how dear you are to me, thank you for your love, help and encouragement.

I would also like to thank all my friends who have encouraged me along the way and were always there to help. Julie Csaki, your editing was incredible.

To all my teachers at Wilder for teaching me everything I know. Without you all, this book would never have been written.

Vincent E. Pilkington-Landreville

# CHAPTER 1

## The Mysterious Book

Joshua was the sort of child who told lies on a regular basis. When his parents would ask him if he had eaten his whole supper, he would say yes. Then, three days later, Joshua's parents would find cabbage hidden under the carpet.

His parents tried to get him to believe that it was not a good idea to lie, because one day, when he would be in trouble and he needed help, no one would come to his aid.

They tried reading to him, *The Boy Who Cried Wolf,* and other stories like *Pinocchio,* but he still did not believe his parents, and therefore, did not change his habits.

Joshua was also a prankster. He put whoopee-cushions on his teacher's chair, and put fake tarantulas in the girls' desks at school.

Joshua was quite well known at school, but unfortunately it wasn't in a good way.

He only had three friends at school, Juliana and Stephanie, two girls that Joshua did not play pranks on, and Erick, a boy who helped Joshua plan his pranks and choose his next victims.

His two older brothers, Jordan and Nicholas, were not much help. They encouraged Joshua to tell lies. They also encouraged him and Erick to play pranks on the teachers and girls in the school.

The most recent "idea" that Jordan and Nicholas had, was to put a bucket of water on the top of each bathroom stall. Then, when someone opened the door, the water would pour onto the unsuspecting victim.

The only reason Joshua did these things, was because if he didn't, no one would pay any attention to him.

One night, when Joshua was in bed, his father came into his room and said, "Joshua, I have decided to read a story to you. The book is long, so I will only read two of the stories in the book. Tomorrow night, if you want, I will continue it."

The book was called *The Story of Stories*. The book was about a young boy who traveled around the world and had adventures; battles with a dragon and ogres, saving a colony of brownies (which are mythological creatures that look like cats) from a giant that didn't watch where he was going (so, he regularly squished brownies with his giant feet), and saving a man from an evil wizard who had tried to eliminate him from the world.

There were more stories in the book, but like his father had said, it was too long to finish that night.

When his father had finished, he kissed Joshua good night and left the room with the book under his arm. Joshua closed his light and fell asleep not long after.

All of a sudden, Joshua woke with a start. He was sweating but he was cold. He looked around his room and there was the book wide open on his dresser. He thought that this was strange since he was positive that he had seen his father leave the room with it.

Joshua took it and began to read. He read about the boy's adventure in Ringadore and about the mummy he had fought in the Pynazim of King Singrand.

Then he read about the enchanted forest the boy had mysteriously found when he was traveling in Africa during the year 1500, and about how he had been attacked by a troll and thousands of grasshoppers.

Joshua loved what he was reading and wished that he could be as heroic as the boy in the story.

He wished he could defeat the ogres and save the brownies from the giant that did not watch where he was going. He wished he could defeat the terrible wizard who had a plan to destroy an innocent man, and battle a mummy in the Pynazim of King Singrand. He wished he could do all the things the boy in the book had done.

For a minute, he forgot that he was in his room and imagined that he was in all the different places that the boy had been to.

Joshua read late into the night and finished the five stories in the book, but he noticed one little detail; at the end of the book, there were ten blank pages.

Joshua thought that this was strange. He flipped through the ten pages. Nothing.

He thought about why there were so many blank pages at the end of the book, but could not come up with a satisfying answer.

Joshua knew that it was normal to have one or two blank pages at the end of a book, but never more than that.

He decided he would ask his father about the blank pages the next day, but before he put the book away, he felt an urge to touch the first blank page for no particular reason.

He lifted his hand, put out his finger, and touched the page.

He started spinning, faster and faster and faster.

The beautiful tapestry his mom had made him was gone, the wall was gone, and even the book disappeared.

Then all of a sudden Joshua was not in his room anymore . . .

# CHAPTER 2

## A New World

Joshua did not like the surroundings of *wherever* he was. Instead of a wall there was an everlasting view, and the air was full of thick grey smoke. To his right was a massive boulder, in back of him was a big black musty cave and to his left was a little golden lake.

Instead of being dull grey and mossy, the boulder was metallic black and scaly.

He said to himself, "This place gives me the creeps! I hope it isn't as bad as it looks."

Joshua did not panic. Instead he shouted, "Hello! Is there anybody here?" There was no answer, but the boulder started to move, and he heard groaning from inside the cave.

"Oh no! What in the world is going on?!" moaned Joshua.

The boulder continued to move and *whatever* was in the cave kept groaning.

Then two huge ugly greenish creatures (which were actually ogres) thundered out of the cave and roared.

The sound was blood-curdling. "It would shatter all the windows around it, if it was where I live!" thought Joshua.

Now Joshua was panicking.

"Arghhh!" roared the monster.

"Ahhhhhhh!" screamed Joshua. He started running in the direction of the boulder. He was about to put his foot on it, only to realize that it was not even there.

He looked up into the sky and there, a huge black and red dragon flew.

The dragon had two yellow eyes and claws as black as night. His entire underbelly was crimson red. His wings were huge and they seemed bat-like.

He had spikes on his tail and on the tips of both of his wings. His teeth were huge, and Joshua could tell even from the distance that they must be bigger and sharper than any shark teeth.

He was breathing fire out of his nose, and Joshua worried that the dragon hadn't eaten in a long time. Joshua had no idea what to do with these three mythological creatures.

"I can't hide in the cave, because who knows what else could be in there, and anyways, the ogres are blocking the way!" said Joshua to himself.

"This is so much like the book!" Joshua thought.


At that moment, everything was clear to him. When he had touched the blank page in the book, he had been drawn into it.

So, Joshua said to himself, "If I am in the book '*The Story of Stories*', I will have the same adventures the boy in the story had. So I have to re-live the adventures he had and perform the exact same tasks that he did to defeat the ogres and the dragon!"

He remembered that the boy in the story had walked to the pond and said something like "rappity-rap". Or was it "ripatty—rip"?

Joshua heard a noise behind him. First, he looked at the ogres. One of them was running in his direction, so Joshua started running the opposite way.

Then he looked at the dragon, it seemed like he was zapping the ground with his fire. That was it! "Zappity-zap" was what the boy had said to the pond!

"Ahhhhhhh!" While Joshua was running to the pond, one of the ogres had grabbed him by his leg and was shaking him as if he were a twig. "What did the boy do? What did the boy do?" Joshua wailed.

After about two minutes of swinging, he felt nauseous, and unfortunately, it was only then that Joshua's "light illuminated". He remembered exactly what his father had read to him. The boy had said five nice things to the ogre.

Joshua started, "Oh! You are such a handsome ogre!" The ogre's eyes opened wide.

Joshua continued, "Ah your eyes! They look like crystals! And your smile, a streak of light from heaven!"

The ogre was surprised that he was getting compliments as nice as these, but he did not let go of Joshua.

Joshua continued in a louder voice, "Your voice is like a beautiful swan singing in the spring time. Your toes are so . . . um . . . well . . . round and shiny?"

This was how Joshua finished, and at that moment, the ogre put him on the ground. Joshua looked back at the dragon that was now flying towards him.

With no hesitation, Joshua ran to the golden lake and said, "Zappity-zap!"

There was a blinding flash of light and then a doorway appeared. Out of the doorway flew a beautiful unicorn.

The unicorn's hair and mane were pure white. Her horn was as silver as money, and her eyes were a beautiful black. Her hooves were also black, not to mention hard as rock.

Unlike the three other creatures, the unicorn spoke in a soft and kind voice.

"Joshua, my name is Alexis. Climb on my back and we will defeat the two ogres and the dragon." Alexis told him.

"But how are we going to defeat them?" Joshua asked.

Alexis looked at Joshua and answered, "You will only see if you climb onto my back."

Joshua looked behind him. The two ogres were charging at him (one of them just realizing that he had been outwitted by a human child) and the dragon had landed and was looking directly at Joshua.

Joshua decided that he would take Alexis' advice, and he said, "Ok, Alexis, I will climb onto your back only if you promise me that we will defeat these terrifying creatures."

Alexis smiled and said, "I promise we will."

Joshua climbed onto Alexis' back. "Are you ready?" Alexis asked.

"Yes, now let's go before we get crushed or turned intooo . . ." Before Joshua finished his sentence, Alexis took off.

She flew right into the first ogre, stabbing him in the stomach with her horn.

The ogre shrieked before he fell to the floor with a big "Thud!" The first ogre was dead.

The second ogre (seeing what had happened to his companion) ran, but Alexis was too fast for him.

She landed on the ogre's head and started tap-dancing. The ogre could not stand the constant banging on his head and he felt like his brain would burst at any second. Unfortunately, the ogre was quite right.

At that exact moment the ogre's head cracked and he fell to the ground like a tree struck by lightning.

The ogre lay in the cave, squirming like a fish out of the sea, and eventually died.

Alexis flew right up to the dragon with Joshua shouting, "Hooray!" and "Yes!" but as soon as he saw the dragon his exclamations turned into, "Oh Oh!" and "No, Alexis! No!"

Alexis ignored Joshua's pleading and started circling the dragon.

The dragon was getting annoyed and dizzy because of Alexis' constant circling.

Fire flared from his nose and his eyes were wide with rage, "How dare you?" he shrieked.

Following Alexis with his eyes, he tried to scorch her and Joshua, but to no avail.

The dragon got dizzy and he fell twenty feet down and hit the ground.

He was lying there, stomach up in the air, taking deep breaths.

"Please don't hurt me, Ms. Unicorn. I was just trying to save my treasure and my children from the human boy. Please don't hurt me!" pleaded the dragon in a hoarse voice.

"Violence is no way to save one's possessions. Even if you have to, it is not the best way. This boy has nothing against you and you have scared him half to death," Alexis scolded.

The dragon looked ashamed of himself, "Oh. Human, I am sorry if I have scared you. I am Ayaren. It is a hard time for me. There is little food in this barren place and my dear children are starving!"

Joshua answered kindly, "I am sorry to hear about your troubles. I wish there was something I could do to help."

When Joshua had finished his discussion with Ayaren, he left him where he was, unharmed.

Joshua climbed back onto Alexis' back and she flew him back to the pond, where the doorway to her home still was.

"Thank you, Alexis for helping me defeat the two ogres, and make a friendship with Ayaren, but how do I get back home?" Joshua said.

"Well, you know the cave that those two ogres came from?" Joshua nodded. "I am sure there is a portal that will bring you right back into your world. Farewell my friend. I hope we meet again," Alexis replied, and then she jumped into the doorway and disappeared.

Joshua was going to complain because he did not want to go into the cave. Who knew if there were more ogres, waiting to tear him limb from limb for what he had done to two of their kindred? The thought made him shudder.

Instead of thinking about these dreadful things, Joshua started walking towards the cave.

When he got to the entrance he murmured, "Here goes nothing!" and walked into the cave.

It was dark in there and it smelled of rotten fish. "This is probably what those foul ogres ate," thought Joshua with a frown on his face.

After a long walk, Joshua spotted a little pool in the middle of the cave. It was bluish yellow.

Joshua suspected that this was the portal, so he jumped in and disappeared.

# CHAPTER 3

# Friends

When Joshua got home after his adventure, he realized that no time had passed since he had left. He was too tired to notice that two of the blank pages were now filled with writing.

"Drrrrrring!" Joshua was at school. He was dying to tell Juliana, Stephanie and Erick about his adventures from the night before.

Joshua couldn't wait to tell his friends about Alexis and the two ogres. He also wanted to tell them how he had met Ayaren and about the sad story Ayaren had told him and Alexis.

Joshua walked into the class and sat down at his desk beside Stephanie.

Stephanie was a tall girl (she was much taller than Joshua) with long blond hair and thin pink lips. She had light blue eyes and round rosy cheeks and she always wore a hair band.

"Psst! Steph, you won't believe what happened to me yesterday!" Joshua whispered.

"What?" asked Stephanie with a doubtful look on her face.

"I touched a blank page in a book and I got sucked into the book and I met a unicorn named Alexis and I killed two ogres with Alexis' help and I met a dragon and . . ." Joshua started.

"Cool! Do you know what I did yesterday? I went to the other side of the world and cut Medusa's head off!" Stephanie answered with a tinge of amusement in her voice.

Joshua was disappointed, "You don't believe me, do you?"

"What do you think Joshua? You're a liar and a prankster. Yes, you're my friend, but how can I believe such an unbelievable story?"

Joshua frowned, "Well . . . If you don't believe me I will . . . I'll . . . go tell Juliana and Erick! They'll believe me!"

Juliana and Erick looked at Joshua skeptically. "How can that be, Joshua?" asked Erick.

"I don't exactly think what we are talking about is possible!" Juliana said, before Joshua could answer.

Joshua nearly cried in frustration. He walked away from his three "friends" and sat down at another table far from Stephanie, Erick and Juliana.

At the end of the day, when Joshua was leaving the schoolyard, Stephanie came up to him.

"Hey Josh, I'm sorry about making you feel bad today. You know I didn't mean it . . ." she said guiltily.

Joshua looked at the ground and said, "Your apology is accepted, but can you at least come and see what I mean?

"The next adventure in the book is saving a colony of brownies from a giant that doesn't watch where he is going. So, that is probably what we are going to have to do next."

Stephanie frowned, "You still don't admit that your *"adventure"* was only a dream, do you?" she said.

Joshua looked up, "It was *not* a dream. It was real. Come, I'll prove it to you!"

As the two friends walked into Joshua's room, Joshua picked up the book.

"This is the book that sucked me into its story!" Joshua told Stephanie, putting his book bag down.

He showed her the book.

"Why are there eight blank pages in it?" Stephanie asked.

"I don't know . . . did you say eight? I thought there were ten. Give me that!"

Stephanie gave Joshua the book. "Hey, this is strange. Yesterday night there were ten blank pages," Joshua began to read. "Oh my . . . This is exactly what happened to me yesterday, you see.

"What I told you about Alexis, and how the dragon became my friend. This is exactly what happened to me last night!"

What had happened to the first two blank pages was very strange indeed.

When Joshua had left the other world through the portal, his adventure had been recorded on the mysterious blank pages.

Joshua did not know that this would be happening at the end of each adventure he had.

Joshua turned to the third blank page and said, "At the count of three, touch the third blank page in the book and you'll see that I've been telling you the truth. One, Two, Three!"

At the same time, Joshua and Stephanie touched the page and they started spinning, faster, and faster, and faster.

The beautiful tapestry his mom had made for him was gone again, the wall was gone and even the book disappeared. Then all of a sudden, they were not in Joshua's room anymore.

# CHAPTER 4

## The Brownie Colony

"Oh my goodness!" shouted Stephanie. "Joshua, where's your room, the wall, the book, and most importantly your house?! Where in the world are we?!" Stephanie was panicking.

"Actually Stephanie, we are not even in our own world. We are in a different place, maybe even on a different planet!

"What I was telling you was all true. Now you can see that for yourself." Joshua said very calmly.

Stephanie was enraged, "THAT is not the point, Joshua! We don't even know where we are!"

Joshua looked around him. He was wondering if Stephanie and he would need to fight the giant to save the brownies.

"Yes, Stephanie, I know where we are. We are in the kingdom of Gerlock. Gerlock is the place where we are going to save some brownies from a giant who always squashes them because he doesn't watch where he is going."

Stephanie frowned and shouted, "So, you're telling me that we have come here, wherever here is, oh sorry 'Gerlock' to save a dessert!"

Joshua laughed, "No. Brownies are little creatures that look like cats. They walk on two legs, like we do, and they eat only one thing; mushrooms!"

This only made Stephanie's face get even redder with anger, "So, we HAVE to save these little mushroom munching creatures from a giant that plans to walk on us!"

"Hey! Don't call me a 'little mushroom munching creature!' You look like one yourself! So there!" a small creature squeaked from the ground.

"Ahhhhhhh! What in the world are these tiny things?!" Stephanie screamed.

Joshua smiled, "Let me introduce you to our first brownie, Stephanie. Excuse me, what is your name?"

The brownie looked suspiciously at Joshua and Stephanie. "Christopher's the name. May I ask you what YOU are?"

Joshua was shocked, "You mean you don't know what I am?"

The brownie looked annoyed, "Exactly! I don't know what you are! Why would I be asking, if I knew?!"

Stephanie was still in shock to see such a little creature speaking, "Joshua, ask him if he's going to hurt us," she whispered.

"Of course I'm not, you silly thing! I'M harmless. You should watch out for the real danger, the giant!"

Stephanie whimpered, "You're scaring me!"

Joshua was still disappointed that Christopher didn't know what sort of "creature" he was, "Well actually, Christopher, I'm a human being and I have come here with my friend to save you from the giant. My name is Joshua."

The brownie had tears of joy in his eyes, "So you've come . . . from wherever you live . . . to save us from the giant?"

Stephanie looked around her, "I'm not planning to stay here for a long time!"

"Well sorry, you are, Steph. We have to help the brownie colony!" Joshua insisted.

Christopher looked surprised, "You know about my colony? I thought the others and I were the only ones to know about our colony!"

Stephanie looked terrified, "There are more of you?"

The brownie rolled his eyes, "How can this boy know everything and you not know a single thing about this place!"

Joshua frowned, "Don't be so rough on her Chris. It's her first time in a different world, and I was the only one to hear the story from the book."

"Oh, sorry, Steaphanie? No, Staphiney? Oh yeah, Stephanie!" the brownie said with difficulty.

"Chris, I don't think she's in the mood for talking right now," Joshua whispered.

The brownie laughed, "Okay guys and gals, it's safe to come out now! I've met the human beans—I mean *beings*, and they seem pretty nice. They want to save us from the giant!"

"Whoa! Mushroom boy! Easy on the 'they'!" Stephanie interjected.

"Yay! Someone is going to save us from the giant! Yay!" came hundreds of little voices.

"OH NO! OH NO! They're coming! Help! Help! They're going to kill me!" shouted Stephanie, while running in circles.

The brownies started giggling, "We're not going to kill you, silly. We're just happy you're going to save us from the giant!"

Stephanie looked in Joshua's direction, "I'm not saving you. He is!" she retorted, pointing at Joshua.

The brownies said, "No! We want both of you to save us!" They all started running towards Stephanie, grabbing her legs.

"Ahhhhhhh!" shouted Stephanie, "Get away from me! Okay! I'll 'save' you from the giant only if you get off of me! Now!"

Joshua was laughing, "Steph! That looked hilarious! They all charged at you!"

Stephanie was upset, "It was not funny being the target, Joshua! How would you feel if a pack of little mushroom munching, furry creatures charged at you?"

Christopher growled, "What did I say about calling us 'mushroom munching creatures', eh?!"

Stephanie looked annoyed, "I am dreadfully sorry you mushroom munching creature," she said under her breath.

Christopher and all the other brownies looked at her, "What was that?" asked Christopher.

"Oh . . . . Um . . . . Nothing important." Stephanie replied.

"Okay then, Joshua and Stoopny, um no, Stephanie, come into our hut and we will have a little chat!"

"I would love to!" Joshua exclaimed.

"Do we have to?" Stephanie inquired, looking worried.

"Yes, Stephanie. Let's go!" Joshua answered with a smile.

# CHAPTER 5

## The Giant

When Joshua finished the conversation with the brownie colony (and a terrified Stephanie), he heard a huge rumbling. "BOOM" "BOOM" "BOOM".

The brownies screamed, "It's the giant! Run everybody! RUN!"

The giant was as huge as the story had said, and he had big reddish eyes. He was definitely not watching where he was going.

He wore a red vest with blue shorts and he was shouting. The sound was like a stampede of elephants, all of them making different sounds. Joshua was actually quite scared. He had to fight *that* giant!

All the brownies ran. Stephanie also started running, but Joshua stopped her, "We have to kill the giant or he's going to squish more than just the trees! He's going to kill the brownies too."

"Are you crazy?! First, you bring us into this different world, and now you are telling me we have to kill a giant who is about one hundred times as big as a man!" Stephanie exaggerated.

"Well we have to, Steph, and he's not *that* big. I wouldn't give him more that twenty-five feet." Joshua gulped. "Do you remember the story of "David and Goliath"?"

"Yes, Joshua! Everyone knows that story! But why do we have to speak about a bible story now? He's going to *squish* us!" Stephanie cried.

"Give me your hair band and some stones! Fast!" Joshua rushed Stephanie.

Stephanie did as she was instructed and Joshua tapped his foot impatiently.

Stephanie ran back to Joshua with three stones and her hair band. He took a branch and put the hair band on it. He took the first stone Stephanie had given him and put it in the middle of the hair band.

"HEADS UP!!!" he shouted to the giant.

The giant looked down at Joshua and Stephanie.

Joshua thought the moment was right. He pulled the hair band back, put the stone in the middle of it and let go. The stone went flying and hit the giant in the middle of the forehead.

At first, the giant did not react, but then he roared as if an anvil had dropped onto his head. He started stomping on the ground.

It felt like there was an earthquake going on. Joshua held onto the nearest tree and Stephanie held onto his leg. Stephanie was screaming, and Joshua was holding on for dear life.

"STOP HIM! STOP HIM, JOSHUA!" Stephanie screeched. Joshua tried his best.


"Giant, stop stomping! You're going to kill everyone! STOP!" Joshua shouted with all his might.

The giant looked down, Joshua tried again. He pulled the hair band back, put the stone in the middle of it and let go.

This time the giant stomped even harder on the ground, and it was like two earthquakes were meeting each other. The ground was shaking so much that Joshua lost his grip on the tree and was thrown into the brownie's hut.

Joshua jumped up, took the sling-shot, pulled the hair band back, put the stone in the middle of it and let go.

The stone hit the giant in the middle of the forehead, and this time, the giant collapsed.

The giant kept falling and within a couple of seconds, he hit the ground. The giant was dead.

# Chapter 6

---

# Rejoice

There was a moment of silence, and then, one of the youngest brownies started clapping. Then all the other brownies, young and old, started clapping and cheering too.

Christopher was sobbing with joy, saying, "Joshua, you killed the giant! Thank you! Thank you!"

Stephanie was standing beside Joshua, with a smile on her face (for the first time that hour) and was patting Joshua on the back.

"I knew you could do it, Joshua! I knew it all along!" Stephanie said.

"Well, without the help of your hair band I wouldn't have been able to do it!" Joshua said with a smile.

"Oh, Joshua, how can we ever repay you?" Chris asked Joshua, still sobbing.

"Well, you can help Stephanie and me to find the portal to get out of this place. You could also let me have one of the rarest mushrooms you have, so that we can convince our friends we have visited a very different place!" Joshua said with a grin.

"Oh, no! You can't leave now! We have only just met, and anyways, you're our hero!" Christopher said, looking a little sad to hear that Joshua was planning to leave.

"Sorry, Chris, we can't. We have to get back home to where we live! Can you please just tell us where the portal is?" asked Joshua, looking a little disappointed himself.

"Well . . . Okay, but we will always remember you and what you did for us! We love you and Stephanie very much!" Christopher said regretfully.

"Thank you, Chris. That is really nice of you. Now where's the portal?" Joshua asked, hoping that Chris would know.

"The portal is in our hut. I am the only one to know about it, since its existence is top secret. Will you follow me?" asked Christopher kindly.

"Yes! We're coming right away! Aren't we, Joshua?!" Stephanie said smiling.

"Yes. Here we come." Joshua answered politely.

They entered the brownie's hut and followed Christopher. Christopher led them into a narrow hallway with a low ceiling. Then, they entered a big room with two pools in it. They both looked like the one Joshua had seen when he had met Alexis and the dragon.

"Thank you, Chris! At the count of three, we must jump together, holding hands," Joshua said to Stephanie, "One, Two, Three!" And they both jumped into one of the pools.

"Noooooo!" they heard faintly as they jumped.

# CHAPTER 7

# The Wrong Portal!

Joshua and Stephanie arrived . . . somewhere.

That somewhere was not Joshua's room. There was a big castle in front of them, and in back of them was a little hidden house in the tattered remains of what looked like vines.

"Joshua, where are we?" Stephanie asked in an impatient and anxious voice.

"I don't know," Joshua said softly, "but it looks like we might be back in medieval times!" he answered calmly.

"Oh great! First we go to brownie world, and now we're back in medieval times!" Stephanie shouted.

"I don't know what went wrong, Steph. We must have taken the wrong portal!" Joshua said, understanding what had happened.

"When we jumped into the first portal, it brought us here. This means we took the wrong portal. It must have brought us directly into the next adventure in the book!" Joshua explained to Stephanie.

"Right, but this is not what I intended to happen! I wanted to go back into *our* world. Not this rundown medieval place!" Stephanie said to Joshua. Unfortunately, she was not as understanding as Joshua was.

"Well, at least we didn't die travelling in the portal." Joshua said optimistically.

"Arghh! No! I want to be back in your room! And in our world!" Stephanie shouted.

"Well, we may as well start walking in the castle's direction. They might tell us where we are and why we are here." Joshua said.

"Oh . . . Okay. Let's go!" Stephanie answered, not quite as enthusiastic as Joshua had hoped.

They started walking in the castle's direction, not noticing that someone was watching them very closely.

On the way to the castle, Joshua was studying the surroundings.

There were a lot of trees (most of them were dead and black), but not many strands of grass, and the only strands that were there were either black or yellow.

At the back of the castle there was a stable which was overflowing with straw, but surprisingly had no animals in it.

"This place seems like it was beautiful once . . ." Joshua said. "I wonder what could have caused it to become such an ugly place." Joshua continued.

"Probably was the giant for all that I know!" answered Stephanie coldly.

"Impossible!" confirmed Joshua. "The giant was in the previous story, and anyways, this place looks like it was damaged by sorcery."

"Yeah right, what do you know about sorcery?" mumbled Stephanie.

"Well, for instance that some sorcery is meant to help people and other sorts are meant to destroy and . . ." Joshua's voice trailed off.

Joshua had stopped talking because he had just seen a shadow behind them, and then it moved.

Joshua swirled around hoping to see what was (or had been) there. There was nothing to be seen.

"Joshua! Hellooo?! What in the world are you looking at?" Stephanie shrieked.

Apparently she was not in a very good mood, nor was she in the mood for stopping in the middle of nowhere.

"Oh . . . Nothing . . . I just saw . . . Whatever." Joshua said, stopping in the middle of each sentence.

"Well then, shouldn't we be moving along?" Stephanie responded coolly.

They continued on their journey. Walking . . . Walking . . . Walking . . . It seemed to take forever, but finally they arrived at the huge castle's entrance.

Joshua turned around positive that he had seen something behind him this time. Then he saw what it was.

It was a man, and he was looking at him through a window in the castle. The man's dishevelled appearance seemed to indicate that he had been locked up in the room for ages and it looked like he was begging Joshua and Stephanie to let him out.

"Stephanie, look up there in the window!" Joshua said, nudging her and not letting his gaze off the man.

Stephanie looked up and said, "Oh my goodness! Look at him! Unfortunately we can't do anything until we're in the castle."

Joshua looked back at Stephanie and said, "Okay then, we'll knock."

"Well, knock then." Stephanie said anxiously.

"Okay . . . Here it goes!" responded Joshua, unsure of himself.

Joshua took the big brass knocker and knocked. Toc, Toc, Toc. The sound was deep and very loud.

Then the door opened with a huge "Creak!"

There stood a man with bloodshot eyes and torn clothes, "Fast, come in before HE follows you!" the man said in a panicked voice.

"Who is HE?" asked Stephanie, startled.

"HIS name is not to be spoken! I am Henry." answered Henry in a scary way.

"Why isn't it?" asked Joshua with a gulp.

"Follow me and you will get your answer!" said Henry in the same tone he had used before.

Stephanie looked at him and said, "By the way, there is a man locked up in a room high in your castle."

"You must have been seeing things. Now follow me!" Henry shouted.

Joshua and Stephanie followed Henry through the dark hallways without a word of protest.

The hallways were lit with torches and the tiles were filthy.

Each corner had its own cobweb, which looked very much like they were glowing in the dark. There were eerie shadows on the walls, and the air was very cold.

And if that was not enough, they could hear a constant "Drip . . . Drip . . . Drip . . ." every three seconds

Henry turned a corner and was gone. Joshua and Stephanie followed. They turned into a room with brown walls and even less torches than in the hallway.

It was very dark in the room, so Joshua and Stephanie did not see the throne in the middle of the room with a man sitting on it.

Unfortunately, they walked straight into the throne and heard the groan of the man who was sitting on it.

The man on the throne groaned again and said, "Please do not kill me! I did not do anything to disturb you!"

"Oh, Master. These children are not here under HIS orders," assured Henry.

"Thank goodness," said the other man with a sigh of relief.

"Now, Master, can you tell them our story?" asked Henry.

"The story is too horrible," moaned the man on the throne, "You tell them, Henry!" he said.

"Yes, Master," Henry responded.

# CHAPTER 8

## The Story

"Well, when my master was a boy, he had an older friend named Carlos . . ."

The man on the throne sighed, "That is HIS name, and what a mistake it was to befriend him . . ."

Henry continued, "Carlos was not a nice boy at all, and for years my master looked up to him. My master did not know that Carlos had powers, powers that could destroy the world with a flick of his finger.

"Because Carlos knew that my master also had these powers, he pretended to be his friend. He decided that if he could receive all of my master's trust, he could drain him of his powers.

"Fortunately, his spell backfired and he was temporarily drained of his own powers.

"Carlos fled to the city of Chrystalyn, which is where we are now, and went into hiding." Henry paused and looked up into the darkness.

Joshua and Stephanie were mesmerized. A few seconds later when Henry hadn't continued, "Well, what happened next?" asked Stephanie.

Henry sighed, "When my master realized that he had been betrayed, he pursued Carlos right to Chrystalyn.

"When we got to Chrystalyn we saw the damage that he had done. We were . . ."

He was cut short by Stephanie, "Wait a minute, how did you get into this picture?"

"Well, while my master was on his way to confront Carlos, he found me in the city of Cermaline, which is also a beautiful city.

"I was poor and I had nowhere to go. My master kindly invited me to come live with him in the castle he had inherited from his great grandfather Vladimir, his grandfather Johannes, and his father Ricardo. You are currently in that very castle.

"Now if you permit me, I will continue our story, and show you around the castle."

Stephanie blushed, "Yes, sorry," she answered, profoundly embarrassed.

"Okay, we were shocked to see what he had done. As you have probably realized, everything outside is in ruins," Stephanie and Joshua nodded. "Yes, well that was all Carlos' work.

"While he was on the run, his powers slowly 'leaked' back into him until they were all back.

"When he got to Chrystalyn, the villagers tried to prevent him from entering the city. He was so upset by their numerous tries to capture him that he summoned a dragon who destroyed the city for him.

"All the villagers fled from Carlos and the city. They were terrified by the magnitude of his power."

"That's horrible!" whispered Stephanie. Joshua realized that this was the first time in a long while that Stephanie hadn't shouted. She was clearly astounded.

"Henry, why are you still in hiding if you don't even know if Carlos is still here?" Joshua asked.

Henry came closer to Joshua and Stephanie and said, "You mean you didn't feel like you were being watched?"

He was so close to Joshua and Stephanie that they could both smell his stale breath.

"When?" Joshua asked in a voice that betrayed his fear.

"While you were coming to the castle," Henry answered very calmly.

The man on the throne looked up and his eyes changed colors. Stephanie did not think this was normal.

Joshua was baffled. How did this man know that he felt like he was being watched all the way to the castle?

"I did!" answered Joshua very nervously.

"Well then HE is still here and HE is on the lookout for my master and me!" said Henry with a shudder.

The man on the throne smiled and said, "Bring them to the dungeons,"

"They have heard too much! Bring them to the dungeons!" he roared, an evil grin illuminating his face.

The man started changing. His face transformed into another man's and the rest of his body did the same. The man's previously blonde hair had turned a greasy jet black and his figure became considerably taller.

"You aren't my master! You're . . . You're Carlos!" Henry shrieked.

"The dungeons," squeaked Stephanie ignoring the fact that the man on the throne was Carlos, "You mean the place where rats and bats scuttle around and there are bones everywhere?!" Stephanie's squeak turned into a shout.

"Yes, that's exactly the place where you are going!" said Carlos. "Now, Henry, bring them down to the dungeons!" he roared.

"But . . . But!" the helpless Henry shouted.

"Do not question me or you will not live to see tomorrow!" cried Carlos.

"Yes. Which cell?" Henry asked, trembling with fright.

"Cell number one hundred twenty-one!" he answered, with a diabolical grin on his face.

"Cell number . . . no, they are just children! You can not put them in such a horrible cell!" screamed Henry.

"I can if I want to!" retorted the evil man.

Stephanie and Joshua were shaking so much you would think they were a broken washing machine.

"Now do as you are told!" Carlos screamed.

"Please not the dungeons! Please not the dungeons!" begged Stephanie.

"Sorry, but I must children. I do not want to die. He will murder me if I do not do as I am told!" said Henry in a shaky voice with the realization that his 'master' was actually Carlos.

"You would be able to come and live with us. Eh, Joshua?!" pleaded Stephanie.

Joshua did not answer.

"Come on, Joshua, he can come with us, can't he?!" Stephanie pleaded.

"No, Stephanie. We can't tell horrible people like these about the portals and the book. We will find a way to get out of this horrid castle . . . sooner or later," Joshua whispered, while Henry led them down the stairs and to the dungeons.

You could almost see the steam pouring out of Stephanie's ears.

"Sooner or later! Sooner or later! Are you insane?!" Stephanie was enraged.

"Shush! Henry will hear you if you don't quiet down!" said Joshua in response to Stephanie's "question".

"Don't you dare tell me to shush-shush! Why don't you yourself?!" Stephanie screamed.

"I'm telling you to shush-shush, or whatever you call it because, first of all we are in a strange castle with two maniacs bringing us to a cell where we are probably going to die. Second of all . . ." Joshua started but was cut off by Stephanie.

"Oh whatever!" she screamed.

They continued walking down the murky stairs, into the unknown.

# CHAPTER 9

## The Dungeons

Henry stopped walking very abruptly. "Here we are. Cell number one hundred twenty-one," he said in an optimistic voice that belied the fact that he was terrified of the place.

"Anyways, who wouldn't be terrified of such a horrible place?" Joshua said to himself trying to calm his racing heartbeat.

"Great! The dungeons! The best place in the world!" Stephanie mumbled.

Henry opened the cell door with a long creak. It sounded as bad as someone scratching a blackboard.

"Here you go, children. This is where you will be . . . er . . . resting for the night!" Henry told Joshua and Stephanie.

"It's okay Henry . . . We already know that this is the place where you are going to let us 'rot in peace'! Very pleasant isn't it, Joshua?" Stephanie said facetiously.

Joshua tried to smile, but found out that it was much too difficult. "Yes . . . very . . ." Joshua said.

"Well in you go!" Henry said, and pushed both children into the cell. He hesitantly started walking towards the throne room. It showed that he feared his meeting with the evil Carlos.

"Bye! Nice meeting you and your foul master who is actually CARLOS!" Stephanie screamed after Henry.

Henry just kept on walking without turning around to say a word.

Joshua was inspecting his surroundings and realized that the cell he was in seemed not to have been cleaned for a great number of years.

There were spider webs all over the walls and there was also a foul stench of something rotting. Joshua did not want to know what it was.

In the corner of the room was a hole in the ground. That was probably where the prisoners went to relieve themselves.

"Fat chance that I use that," Joshua thought.

On the wall was a small window, barely letting any light into the cell.

Joshua wondered why Henry was so scared of this place other than the fact that this was jail. The real deal.

Stephanie was sitting on the floor and was saying, "Why me of all the people in the world, why me?!"

For the first time, Joshua lost his temper and cried, "You are actually THE LUCKIEST person in our world to be travelling into worlds unknown! I know many other people that would love to be here and they aren't as ungrateful as you are!"

Stephanie was shocked. Joshua had never spoken to her like that! Never! Now that she thought about it, Joshua was always kind with her.

"Sorry, Joshua," Stephanie murmured.

"Okay, but don't be so ungrateful!" Joshua said, still fuming.

"Okay. I won't," Stephanie said, "At least I'll try! Because those brownies and that horrible story and this and that are too much to handle! Really, those brownies are so crazy! And that man! He's diabolical!" Stephanie shouted.

"I agree," Joshua said hoarsely, "Now let's get to business and find our way out of here!"

"Let's do it!" shouted Stephanie.

"Shhh!" said Joshua in answer.

"Why should I be quiet?! Eh?!" Stephanie shouted.

"We had an agreement, didn't we?" Joshua snapped back.

"OH . . . Right! Sorry. I forgot! Oops," Stephanie answered more quietly than before.

Joshua smiled. He'd never been rough with Stephanie, but when he did, he guessed it worked better than being too calm. That probably just made Stephanie go nuts.

"Now . . . how do we get out of here?" Stephanie asked Joshua.


"We could try to break the window over there on the wall. That's probably the only way to get out of this dump, so I guess we could try," Joshua said more to himself than to Stephanie.

"Then let's DO IT!" shouted Stephanie.

Joshua just had to look at Stephanie and she lowered her voice.

"Let's go," Stephanie whispered, fearing that Joshua would snap at her again.

Joshua looked around trying to find something to break open the window. He found something, but unfortunately it was in the worst place possible. The toilet.

"Uhh . . . Stephanie, do you mind getting that piece of metal in the . . ." Joshua started.

"Toilet," screamed Stephanie. "You want me to get a stupid piece of metal in the . . ."

"Toilet . . . yes I do!" Joshua answered nervously.

"What's MY reward for this gross task? Huh?" asked Stephanie.

"You'll be able to get out of this prison," Joshua said confidently.

"Ohh . . . Okay I'll do it for . . ." Stephanie answered, but was cut off by Joshua.

"Thank you so much . . . now please do it," Joshua responded.

"Okay . . . Now?" asked Stephanie very squeamishly.

"Um . . . Yeah, now!" answered Joshua calmly.


Stephanie started walking towards the toilet, saying, "I am now advancing towards the toilet. I am two steps away from the toilet. I am reaching into the toilet, and picking up this filthy piece of metal!"

Joshua smiled and took the piece of metal from Stephanie. He walked towards the small window and cracked it open.

All of a sudden, the floor disappeared under Joshua and Stephanie's feet.

"Ahhhhh!" screamed Stephanie, as they plummeted through the dark hole that used to be the floor.

Joshua also screamed, if possible even louder than Stephanie, terrified of what had just happened.

Joshua hit the floor, landing more heavily on one foot than the other, "Oww!" he shrieked.

The room was so dark that Joshua couldn't see anything at all.

Beside him landed Stephanie with an equally heavy thud and, "OWW!" she hollered.

Joshua reached for his ankle to see if he had broken anything. Thankfully, he couldn't detect anything wrong, but it still hurt. Perhaps it was only a sprain.

"Stephanie, my foot's banged up!" he said weakly.

Stephanie reached down to check hers.

"Mine is okay," she said, "But I think I hurt my wrist."


"Can you try to get up?" Joshua asked Stephanie nervously, hoping that she could.

"I'll do my best!" she answered.

Joshua let out a gasp when he felt something tug on his arm.

"It's only me," said Stephanie, before Joshua could even ask.

"Thank goodness. I thought that . . ." suddenly Joshua felt a tug on the ankle that he hadn't landed on.

"Tell me that it's you tugging on my ankle!" Joshua begged.

Stephanie looked nervously at Joshua's ankle just to realise that she couldn't see it.

"It's not me . . ." Stephanie said shakily.

"Oh no . . ." said Joshua.

Whatever was holding onto Joshua's ankle kept tugging, and then all of a sudden, he was pulled into a pool of freezing water.

# CHAPTER 10

# The Pool of Water

Joshua tried to pull his leg away from the person or thing holding him, but with no luck.

Whatever was pulling him down was also pulling Stephanie, since she was still holding onto Joshua's arm.

Down they went, struggling to free themselves from the deathly grip.

"Arrrgg!" sputtered Joshua as he finally fell on hard ground.

"Awww!" sputtered Stephanie as she also hit the ground.

"Ha, ha, ha!" someone laughed.

Joshua did not even have to look up to see who it was. He'd recognize that laugh anywhere.

"Carlos!" shouted Stephanie, enraged and soaking wet.

"Well, well, well! How did you guess?" he said mockingly.

"You rat headed . . ." Stephanie started under her breath.

Joshua looked at Carlos and said, "How dare you drag us down here?!"

"What did you expect? That was cell number one hundred twenty-one!" Carlos roared with laughter.

"What did it do to us other than bring us to your chambers?" asked Joshua questioningly.

"Nothing, except introduce you to my friend the Quanago!" he screamed happily.

"A Quana-what?" asked Stephanie uncomprehendingly.

"The Quanago! He will only rip you limb from limb, so don't run away!" he answered cruelly.

"Show us the portal!" screamed Stephanie.

Carlos, confused said, "What is a portal?"

Stephanie, horrified, looked at Joshua pleading to have misheard Carlos' confusion. Joshua shook his head miserably.

Then, all of a sudden, out of nowhere appeared a horrible looking beast. Actually, it flew out of nowhere.

It was a big beast with a fish head and a bird body. It had a long tail with a stinger at the end of it. Like a fish, it was scaly.

It had a multitude of differently sized spikes on its breast, making it look even more fearsome.

It let out a horrifying scream as it flew towards Joshua and Stephanie. It was the Quanago.

"Ahhh!" shrieked Stephanie as the Quanago picked her up with its claws.

Joshua jumped into action, surprising himself—his foot didn't hurt anymore—and looked around to see if he could use anything to hit the Quanago. Nothing was in sight. He'd have to use his hands and feet.

He ran towards the Quanago with a battle cry and kicked the shrieking creature on its wing.

The Quanago turned towards Joshua and let out another shriek. It picked Joshua up, dropping Stephanie at the same time.

Stephanie scrambled out of the Quanago's way, leaving Joshua to deal with it.

"Ha, ha, ha!" Carlos laughed, watching the whole spectacle unfold.

Stephanie shrieked and ran towards Carlos.

Joshua knew that this was a mistake, since Carlos was a magic user, but he had his own problems to deal with.

Joshua struggled to free himself from the Quanago's grip, and realized that this was probably the creature that dragged him down here in the first place. This gave Joshua the urge to fight.

Joshua kicked the Quanago in the chest and gasped in pain. The Quanago's chest was as hard as rock.

Meanwhile, Stephanie kept running towards Carlos. She was so stressed and angered at being dragged into these worlds that she had to take it out on someone.

Carlos laughed, raised his wand and said, "*Stope Incartius!*"

Fortunately, nothing else happened to Joshua, but Stephanie's legs buckled and she fell to the ground with a thud.

"You imbecile!" screamed Carlos. "You thought that you could match my great powers of magic?"

"I would have if you hadn't cast that dumb spell on me!" shrieked Stephanie.

"Even without my powers, you are no match for me!" Carlos said confidently, tossing his wand to the ground.

"Let's see how you do now!" she screamed and jumped back to her feet.

She ran right to Carlos and shoved him to the ground.

"How could a young girl like you muster up such force?" Carlos asked, fearing that he had underestimated her.

"Four years on the girls' rugby team!" Stephanie answered proudly.

"Oww!" screamed Joshua as the Quanago bit him on the leg.

Vincent E. Pilkington-Landreville

"Argh!" the Quanago roared.

"Joshua, try to outsmart him," shouted Stephanie, "Use his force to your advantage!"

"How?" asked Joshua in pain.

"Get him to use his stinger!" Stephanie screeched.

"Get him to use his stinger!" mimicked Carlos as he scrambled for his wand.

To stop him, Stephanie kicked him in the chin. "Three years in karate!" she said to the now unconscious Carlos.


Joshua looked at the Quanago's stinger and thought of how he could use it. He thought of the book and what the amazing boy had done.

Then it hit him. The Quanago was attracted to bright colors and stung anything that was bright.

Joshua looked at his clothes and noticed that he had red socks on.

'Here goes nothing,' Joshua thought.

He kicked off his shoe and pulled off his sock. He took the sock and thrust it onto one of the spikes on the Quanago's chest.

The Quanago released Joshua and lashed out at his chest, attempting to rid himself of the red nuisance. In doing so, he pierced his chest. The poison quickly flowed to the Quanago's heart, and then he fell.

Joshua let out a sigh of relief and ran to Stephanie and Carlos.

"Thank goodness!" Stephanie sighed, relieved that the Quanago was finally taken care of.

Joshua stood beside Stephanie and said, "We need to get out of here right away!"

"I agree," said Stephanie, "But shouldn't we put Carlos in a cell, so that he doesn't escape?"

52

"That'd be a good idea, considering that he's a maniac!" said Joshua.

All of a sudden, someone said, "You children are certainly right."

"Did you say that?" Joshua asked Stephanie.

"No it was me, Henry," said Henry, stepping out of the shadows.

"YOU!" screamed Stephanie, enraged that he dared show himself in front of her.

She started running towards Henry, but Joshua stopped her, "Maybe he can help us with Carlos."

"Indeed I can," said Henry, "Just follow me."

Stephanie hesitated and said, "Wait a minute . . . my companion and I must have a discussion before we leave."

"Of course . . ." acknowledged Henry.

"Yes . . ." Stephanie pulled Joshua aside and whispered, "So you're telling me to follow this wacko's servant?!" she said pointing at the unconscious Carlos.

"He's our only hope to find out how to lock Carlos up and go back home. I suggest we try it!" Joshua answered.

"Well, if you put it that way, I guess we should . . ." Stephanie started.

"Great! Henry, show us the way!" Joshua said enthusiastically.

"I see you have agreed upon following me!" Henry said cheerily.

"Well, what are we waiting for?" asked Stephanie.

"We must remove Carlos' body from here, or else he will escape and wreak havoc. Is that a good enough reason for you to wait?" Henry asked Stephanie.

"Of course . . ." Stephanie said, blushing furiously.

"Now . . . who will move his body?" asked Joshua nervously.

"I guess I will have to move him," Henry moaned.

Joshua sighed in relief, thinking of how hard it would have been to drag Carlos . . . wherever they were going.

"Henry . . . where are we going to bring Carlos?" Joshua interrogated.

"A secret stairway that my mast—um Carlos and I discovered," Henry retorted.

"Can we go . . . now?" questioned Stephanie, getting impatient.

"As soon as I get Carlos onto my shoulders," Henry answered.

Henry lifted Carlos and put him on his shoulders, signalling Joshua and Stephanie to come with him.

The children started walking, Henry trudging in back of them.

Joshua and Stephanie slowed down, realizing that Henry was far behind them, and they didn't know where they were going.

Joshua smiled and slowed down even more so that Henry could catch up with them.

Henry caught up with the children and pointed them in the direction of a door.

On the door were the words:

*Secret Door*

*Discovered by Henry Jalkins*

*And*

*Master*

*On*

*December 30th 1983*

"Not so secret, huh?" Stephanie inquired.

Henry laughed and said, "My master insisted that we put this on the door!"

Henry opened the door and peered inside, "Nothing!"

"What do you mean, 'nothing'?" asked Stephanie edgily.

"Well . . . I suspect you don't really want to know," Henry answered, chuckling nervously.

"I guess not," said Joshua, smelling the stale air coming from the doorway.

"Well, up we go!" Henry said in a singsong voice.

"Well up we go . . ." parroted Stephanie with no enthusiasm.

Henry and Stephanie started up the stairs, not wasting a second.

Joshua shot a last glance behind him, and started climbing into the dingy darkness.

# CHAPTER 11

## The Dark Staircase

"Wait for me!" Joshua cried, as he ran up the staircase.

"Bah! You better hurry up because *I'm* not waiting for you! It's taking us long enough without you slowing us down!" Stephanie howled.

Her voice echoed in the steep staircase.

Joshua ran up the staircase, trying to catch up with Stephanie and Henry who'd left him behind in their dust. Literally.

Suddenly, the ground started to rumble and an avalanche of rocks fell, not a metre behind Joshua.

"What was that?" Stephanie asked nervously.

"Oh, only five tons of rocks falling behind me!" Joshua stated coolly.

"What?!" shouted both Stephanie and Henry simultaneously. Henry and Stephanie, spun around and stared at Joshua, wide-eyed.

"Just like I said; five tons of rocks falling down behind me!" he said impatiently, finally catching up with the duo.

"Can we go now?" asked Stephanie nervously.


"Can we go now?" Joshua repeated under his breath mockingly.

Stephanie laughed sarcastically and said, "Let's go . . . NOW!"

Henry nodded in agreement.

The trio continued up the staircase in dead silence. No one spoke a word in fear of causing another avalanche.

They finally came to a big pair of wooden doors marked:

*End of Staircase*

*Feel free to look around!*

"Feel free to look around," muttered Stephanie, "Ha! Let's kill ourselves instead!"

"Um . . . let's go now. Through this door is the passage to the magic proof cells," Henry said nervously.

Henry pushed on the doors and they opened without a sound.

Henry grunted with the effort since he was still holding Carlos.

Joshua and Stephanie walked through the doors and gasped in wonder.

They had just walked into a huge glass room, with glass cells everywhere.

The most incredible thing was the ceiling. It too was made of glass, but incredibly, someone had painted marvellous pictures of people in dark robes somehow making dragons appear out of thin air.

Henry walked in and said, "This is where we will be keeping Carlos. All the glass in this room is enchanted, so no one will be able to penetrate, or get out of this room."

"Wow!" whispered Stephanie unbelievingly.

Henry walked towards one of the cells, opened the door and dumped Carlos inside. He closed the door, and was about to lock it when . . .

"Wait please!" someone shouted.

This made Stephanie, Joshua and Henry all jump.

Someone jumped out of the cell into Henry's arms.

"Master!" Henry shouted joyfully

"Yes, it's me! This beast that you just dumped into the cell with me locked me up in here! Now, I have finally been freed from this horrible prison cell!" Henry's master said.

"I am so happy to see you, Master! When I realized that you were Carlos . . . sorry, he was Carlos, I was devastated. I thought he had killed you!" Henry said.

Henry's master looked at Joshua and Stephanie and said, "Yes, thank you very much. Now I think it's about time we send these children back home. Follow me!"

He walked towards the cell beside Carlos' and Stephanie and Joshua followed him.

Henry's master smiled and pointed to four portals on the ground.

"Which one brings us back home?" inquired Joshua, not wanting to have another adventure too soon.

Henry's master looked at the portals and said, "The first one. Remember that the first one will always bring you to where you seek."

"Okay . . . Joshua, can we go now?" Stephanie asked pleadingly.

Joshua looked up and said, "Of course . . . thank you Henry, you have helped us a lot. Thanks Master, for leading us to the portals."

Stephanie took Joshua's hand and said, "One, two, three, JUMP!"

"We will both see you soon!" Henry cried.

"'Till next time!" shouted Henry's master.

"What do you mean?" shrieked Joshua.

Before Henry answered, they both were gone.

Henry sighed and said, "I'll miss those children . . ."

# CHAPTER 12

## Out of the Darkness

Stephanie opened her eyes and sighed in relief, "Home . . ."

Joshua let out his breath, opened his eyes and fell on his bed glad to be in familiar surroundings.

"I wonder what time it is . . . we must have been gone for at least thirty-six hours!" Stephanie exclaimed.

Joshua pointed at the clock on his dresser and said, "No time has passed since we left."

Stephanie gasped, "Then what recorded our journeys?"

Joshua, remembering the book, got off his bed and walked slowly towards it. He reached out and took the book in his hands.

"What are you doing?" asked Stephanie cautiously.

"Just checking something . . ." he answered.

Joshua looked at the last pages in the book and gasped, "Everything's recorded. Here's me killing the giant and Stephanie, screaming her head off in the dungeons!"

"Really! Let me see that!" Stephanie said, tearing the book out of Joshua's hands.

"Wow!" she said, amazed by Joshua's discovery.

Joshua's mom was walking down the hallway when she saw Stephanie and Joshua in his room and said, "Joshua! Did I ever give you permission to have friends over after school?"

Joshua looked at the floor and said, "No . . . but you have to see what we did!"

Joshua's mom rolled her eyes and muttered, "Probably some other dumb joke of yours."

Even though she disapproved of what Joshua was probably going to show her, she walked into the room and sat on her son's bed.

Joshua brought the book to his mom and pointed at the pages in it and said, "Look at this."

Joshua's mom looked hesitantly at the book and smiled, "How interesting, you guys have been writing a book together."

"Actually, we haven't been the ones writing this . . . It was written when we went to Brownie World and Chrystalyn. Wasn't it, Joshua?" Stephanie explained.

Joshua looked at his mom and said, "Stephanie's right, mom. This book has been sucking us into different places and trust me, it's weird."

Joshua's mom laughed and exclaimed, "Boy, you guys do have imagination!"

Stephanie looked like she was about to burst, but Joshua nudged her in the ribs before she could say anything.

"You're right, mom . . . what we said is just our book's plot!" Joshua said, disappointed that his mother didn't believe him.

Joshua's mother smiled and said, "Okay then, I'll let you guys work on this together. You have thirty minutes, then Stephanie has to go home."

Joshua's mother walked out of the room smiling, relieved that Joshua hadn't called her so that she could be the victim of one of his mischievous pranks.

"WHAT?!" screamed Stephanie when Joshua's mom was far away from the room.

Joshua looked at the ground and said, "She didn't believe us, that's all. It's mostly my fault, since I lie so much."

Stephanie, seeing Joshua so upset, frowned and walked towards him. Stephanie looked at Joshua and said, "Oh, Joshua, don't feel bad. It's not your fault. It's just that it's too unbelievable."

Joshua looked up hopefully and said, "You really think that it's just that?"

"Of course!" said Stephanie cheerfully.

"Good," Joshua said relieved, "Now let's go on our next adventure!"

Stephanie's mouth dropped into an 'O' shape, "Y-You mean now?!"

"Of course! If we have to have all the adventures in the book, we may as well have them now!" said Joshua.

"No! I d-don't want to! It's crazy! We just came back from nearly getting killed and you want us to go back into this devil of a book, so that it can take advantage of us again?! Nuh-huh!" Stephanie said, getting very worked up.

"Okay, then! I'll go alone!" Joshua said, getting hard-headed.

Stephanie looked at Joshua saying, "You can't go without me. I just want to wait until tomorrow. I've had enough adventures for one day."

Joshua smiled and said, "Okay then. You win. I'll study the next adventure and find out if we'll need anything."

"Good plan! See you tomorrow!" Stephanie said, heading out the door.

Joshua said good bye, and re-read the story right after the one that took place in Chrystalyn. He discovered that he really did like reading, and also found out about a couple of items that would be useful the next day.

They would need two water bottles, two flashlights, some food, and lots of rope. Joshua knew that Stephanie and he would probably be there for a pretty long time. They were going to Ringadore!


It was Saturday. Joshua and Stephanie would have the whole day to go on their adventures.

Stephanie got there early that morning, and walked into Joshua's room.


"Joshua will be out of the washroom in a minute, Stephanie. He's just getting washed up. Have fun!" Joshua's mother said, smiling.

Stephanie sat on Joshua's bed waiting for him to finish. The door to the washroom opened and Joshua walked out.

"Hi, Joshua! Ready to put ourselves in needless peril once again?!" was Stephanie's greeting.

"Yeah! Something like that!" Joshua responded.

"Right . . ." Stephanie replied.

Joshua nodded and said, "Uh huh . . . Now let's go. I have everything we need right here in my backpack."

"Okay. Is there anything else we need?" Stephanie asked nervously.

"I don't think so . . . Do you need to go to the washroom?" Joshua answered by asking a question.

"I don't need to go!" Stephanie answered ingignantly.

"Good! Then let's go!" Joshua said, "On the count of three. One, two, three!"

They both touched the page of the book that Joshua had just taken from his seldom-used library, and were gone.

# CHAPTER 13

## The Pynazims

"Amazing!" Stephanie gasped in wonder.

Joshua opened his eyes to see that Stephanie was right. The scene was spectacular. Even though Joshua was half blinded by the suns reflecting off the sand, he kept his eyes open. Yes, suns. There were four suns in the sky!

The sand he was walking on was burning hot. He could even feel it through his shoes!

In front of him were three humongous, pyramid-shaped objects. *"Ah . . . So these must be the pynazims."* Joshua thought.

The one that attracted most of his attention was The Pynazim of King Singrand. It was gleaming in the sunlight, and was even brighter than the sand.

The other pynazims, The Pynazim of Cratiera and The Pynazim of Leltrand stood majestically on both sides of The Pynazim of King Singrand.

The Pynazim of King Singrand was the one that captured Joshua's attention the most. It was enormous, standing almost twice as high as the two other pynazims. He knew that this was where Stephanie and he would have to fight the mummy of King Singrand. Hopefully, they wouldn't lose!

"Oh my gosh! We're going to have fun here!" Stephanie said happily.

Joshua decided that it was time to tell Stephanie why they were really here, "Um, Stephanie. The reason we are here isn't to have fun. We're going to fight a mummy."

Stephanie slowly turned her head, and looked at Joshua incredulously, "Why didn't you tell me this *before* we got here?!"

"I knew you wouldn't come with me if you had known what we were really going to do!" Joshua answered.

"B-But I don't want to fight a mummy! We're in Egypt and we're supposed to have fun here!" Stephanie complained.

Joshua winced and said, "Oh . . . There's another thing. We're not in Egypt, we're in Ringadore."

"Ringadore! Are you kidding? We're in another world!" Stephanie shouted.

Joshua stared at Stephanie and said, "I'm not kidding. We're not in Egypt or on Earth for that matter. We're on planet Inkergun."

"INKERGUN! Have you totally lost your mind?! That's not even a planet!" howled Stephanie miserably.

Joshua rolled his eyes and started walking towards the pynazim.

Stephanie looked at Joshua walking away and said, "Wait for me! Even though I don't necessarily want to be here, I'll help you."

Joshua stopped midway to the Pynazim and turned around, "So you aren't going to stay here waiting for me?" he said mockingly, knowing that she wouldn't have dared.

"Yes, I'll come!" she said grudgingly, "But it doesn't mean I want to be here, you know!"

"I already figured that out!" said Joshua, annoyed.

Stephanie stayed with Joshua and they finished their walk towards the pynazim.

Stephanie was amazed to see that the pynazim was made out of metal, but it reflected the color of the sand. This 'pynazim' was probably going to be much different than a pyramid in their world.

Joshua walked towards the pynazim and touched it. A surge of electricity rushed through his body and he screamed in shock.

"Oh my goodness! What's happened to you?!" Stephanie screamed, as equally shocked as Joshua was.

"Oh, I forgot that the pynazim was protected by a fence of electricity that no one can see. I was foolish enough to touch the pynazim, so I was electrified!" Joshua said, rubbing his hand.

"This is crazy!" Stephanie complained, "How are we supposed to get in if we'll be blasted into oblivion, if we so much as touch this hunk of metal?"

Joshua thought about the book and said, "I remember that there was this special lever that can open a door invisible to the naked eye."

"Oh fun!" Stephanie said sarcastically, "So we have to find an invisible lever that will open an invisible door to this . . . uh?"

"Pynazim! Why can't you remember such a simple name?" Joshua complained.

"The only reason you'd remember that is if you're a bookworm!" Stephanie answered, walking away in a huff.

Stephanie was a couple of steps away from the pynazim when she tripped. What had she tripped over? The lever!

"Thanks, Stephanie! You found the lever!" said Joshua, laughing.

Stephanie looked at the lever and said, "Uh-huh. But I thought it was invisible!"

"It is until someone touches it," Joshua explained.

Joshua walked over to the lever and pulled it down. All of a sudden, a huge door opened wide without a sound.

"Wow!" gawked Stephanie, looking up at the huge door.

"Well, let's go in!" Joshua said, not wasting a second.

"Are you sure we should?" Stephanie asked, the anxiety showing in her voice.

Joshua considered the question and said, "Yes, we should."

So they walked into the Pynazim . . . into the deadly silence.

# Chapter 14

# Into the Pynazim

The room they were in was lit by a dim light coming from the side wall. They looked down the metallic hallway, and saw that it was faintly, or not lit at all.

Stephanie gulped and said, "I should have never found that lever."

Joshua looked at her and said, "You didn't find the lever. You tripped over it, then *I* saw it!" he argued.

"Whatever! We shouldn't be arguing at a time like this, you know!" Stephanie said, not raising her voice above a whisper.

Joshua walked over to the light on the wall and said, "You're right. Sorry!"

"Right. Where are we going to go now?" asked Stephanie walking over to Joshua.

When Joshua had finished inspecting the light he said, "We have to go down the hallway. There are going to be traps, so we'll have to be careful."

"Okay then, let's go . . ." Stephanie said, trailing off in fear.

Stephanie started running towards the second light when, "NO!" screamed Joshua.

Stephanie froze in mid-step and walked back a couple of steps.

"What is wrong with you?!" Joshua yelled. "You nearly got both of us killed!"

"How?" Stephanie asked confused.

"The metal plates you were about to step on are traps! As soon as you walk on them, the ground collapses. You don't want to go through that again, do you?" Joshua asked.

"No way!" Stephanie answered, shuddering at the mere thought of what had happened to them in Chrystalyn.

Joshua nodded and said, "I didn't think so."

"Now we have to find a way to get across this trap!" Stephanie said.

"Yes, we do. Do you have any ideas how to get across?" asked Joshua, looking at Stephanie.

"Well, before we left you told me that you were bringing ropes. Maybe that could help!" Stephanie said smiling.

"What do you want us to do, Tarzan across the pit?" Joshua asked complaining.

Stephanie smiled and nodded.

Joshua just had to look at her to know that she thought this was a good idea. A huge smile covered his face and he said, "You *are* crazy!" and gave Stephanie the rope.

Stephanie took the rope and looked at the ceiling. There was a light fixture on the ceiling that looked sturdy enough to hold a lot of weight.

Stephanie knotted the rope to make a lasso and threw it at the fixture.

It wrapped around perfectly.

"Voila!" said Stephanie proudly. She took the rope and swung over the traps.

"Your turn!" Stephanie said, swinging the rope back across to Joshua.

Joshua gulped, took the rope, and swung across without a problem.

"Good job!" exclaimed Stephanie, relieved that they had made it.

"Thank you!" Joshua answered, also relieved.

"Now, where do we go and where is the next trap?" asked Stephanie, scared that they might be standing on the trap at that exact moment.

"The next trap is close to the tomb. It's not going to be as easy as you might think though . . ." Joshua answered.

"What do you mean?" asked Stephanie nervously.

"Never mind . . ." Joshua trailed off.

"Okay! We should be moving on, don't you think?" Stephanie said.

"Yes, of course!" answered Joshua, coming out of his trance.

Joshua and Stephanie started walking down the hallway when they heard a strange chirping sound. They looked around, but saw nothing.

"What do you think it is?" asked Stephanie jumpily.

"I don't know . . . Oh shoot! The micro-monsters!" Joshua shouted.

"What are those?" asked Stephanie.

"RUN!" screamed Joshua, taking off as fast as he could.

Stephanie was hot on his tail, not wanting to be left behind with these things.

The chirping kept getting louder when all of a sudden, a small metallic thing jumped onto Stephanie. It started gnawing at her neck with sharp teeth.

"Ahh! A MICRO-CHIRPER!" screamed Stephanie, finally realizing that these were the micro-*monsters* Joshua had been talking about.

"Stephanie! Pull it out of your hair fast!" Joshua screamed, nearly out of breath. The micro-monsters were still flying right behind them.

The micro-monster thrashed in Stephanie's hair. She pulled frantically, trying to get it out.

"What in the world! You said that the next trap was at the tomb, Joshua!" Stephanie shrieked, as she finally got the micro-monster out of her hair.

All the other micro-monsters had disappeared, to who knows where.

"Stephanie, don't you realize? We have reached the tomb!" Joshua answered seriously.

"Oh!" Stephanie answered unenthusiastically.

In front of them was a huge sheet of metal that was the door to the tomb.

"Is that the door?" asked Stephanie in awe.

"Probably. Now to get in . . ." said Joshua.

"That door is huge! We'll never be able to move it!" complained Stephanie.

"Well, we have two choices, Stephanie." Joshua started. "One, find out how to open the door, fight the mummy, and find the portal. Two, stay here for the rest of our lives. Which one do you prefer?"

"Neither!" Stephanie answered.

"Okay then . . ." Joshua said not paying attention.

"Argh!" Stephanie grunted.

"Uh-huh . . ." Joshua said, looking around the door trying to find something that might open it.

Stephanie sat down, bored, "When are you going to be done?"

"It depends if I find anything!" answered Joshua irritably.

"Ah! I am *totally* dying of boredom!" Stephanie complained.

"Shut up!" shouted Joshua, stomping his foot on the floor.

The Pynazim echoed, and then all of a sudden the door to the tomb opened.

Both Stephanie and Joshua choked on the dust and stale air pouring out of the tomb.

"Do we really have to go in there?" asked Stephanie, still choking.

"We have to if we want to fight the mummy, you know . . ." answered Joshua hesitantly.

"Well, well, well! Look at who seems to be scared of going into the tomb!" Stephanie mocked Joshua.

"I'm not afraid! It's just the air in there seems impossible to breathe from what we have discovered so far!" Joshua answered unconvincingly.

"*Right!*" Stephanie said, rolling her eyes.

Joshua shot Stephanie a look and said, "Be quiet and let's go into the tomb."

"Okay then . . ." Stephanie answered, looking into the doorway.

Joshua walked into the tomb and looked behind him to see that Stephanie was following, trying to prove herself to Joshua.

Joshua looked at the far wall. It was full of dust, and grime. The room wasn't lighted at all, and neither were the three hallways leading away from the entrance to the tomb.

"So . . . where do we go?" inquired Stephanie.

Joshua looked at Stephanie, who was standing beside him and said, "According to the book, we should take the left hallway."

"The left . . . What is so special about the left hallway?" Stephanie asked.

"The mummy is going to be there in his coffin hidden by a metal wall. We're going to have to find another lever, or maybe the mummy will be waiting for us . . ." Joshua said looking down the left hallway.

"What do you mean he might be waiting for us?" asked Stephanie looking at Joshua questioningly.

"He might be out of his metal coffin . . ." Joshua answered, finally tearing his gaze away from the hallway.

"Why would he be?" asked Stephanie, starting to panic.

"Because he might already be awake," Joshua answered.

"Why would he be awake?" asked Stephanie, her panic rising.

"Stop asking questions! We should be down that hallway and fighting the mummy by now!" Joshua said annoyed.

"Okay . . . but I'm scared!" Stephanie said terrified.

"I can tell, but we have to go or we are going to have to stay here in this tomb and wait until we die!" Joshua said laying out their choices.

"Oh, okay, you win!" Stephanie said grudgingly.

The two nervous friends started down the left hallway, not realizing that something was following them.

# CHAPTER 15

## Down the Hallway

The hallway was also full of dust, coming up in little clouds as Joshua and Stephanie walked by.

Their footsteps echoed eerily through the hallway, making Stephanie cringe.

"This is nuts! The mummy is going to hear us, if we keep making so much noise!" Stephanie complained.

"He may as well! I want to get this over with and get back home!" Joshua retorted.

"I thought *you* were the brave one!" Stephanie said frowning.

"I am . . . it's just this is really unnerving!" Joshua answered, looking at Stephanie as they continued down the hallway.

Finally, they reached a large, empty room. Joshua looked around and saw . . . more dust.

"What are we supposed to do now?" whispered Stephanie.

Joshua looked back at Stephanie and said, "We have to find the mummy's coffin."

"What are we waiting for then?" Stephanie said, eager to get out of this place.

"We have to find the lever first," Joshua answered, looking for signs of the lever.

Both Stephanie and Joshua walked farther into the room and started inspecting the walls. Joshua found nothing. Neither did Stephanie.

"Uh! I can't find anything!" Stephanie said impatiently.

Joshua turned around to speak when he saw something right behind Stephanie. A lever.

Joshua kept his eyes on the lever and said, "Stephanie, don't move."

"Why not?" asked Stephanie stubbornly, though she didn't move.

"Because the lever is right behind you!" Joshua answered calmly, walking towards Stephanie.

"Finally we've found something without it being a complete accident!" Stephanie muttered crossly.

Joshua walked towards the lever that was almost blending in with the wall, and pulled down. For an instant nothing happened, and then a section of the wall started to rise.

"Wow! So . . . the mummy is in there?" inquired Stephanie.

"He's supposed to be . . . ." answered Joshua fearfully.

"Is there something else that you haven't told me yet?" asked Stephanie, fearing the worst.


"Actually there is . . . If the mummy isn't in his coffin, the book said that he is prowling around the Pynazim watching us . . . ." Joshua answered shakily.

"Well then . . . let's hope that he's in his coffin!" Stephanie said, turning pale.

The door continued its ascent as Stephanie and Joshua stared at it, willing it to hurry up.

They were scared of what they might find, and absolutely terrified of what they might not find.

When the door finally stopped moving, Joshua said, "We'll have to open the coffin sooner or later, so why don't we do it now?"

"Because my bones are frozen and you would have to use a crane to move me!" Stephanie muttered.

"I'm scared too, Stephanie, but if we don't do this, we'll never be able to get back home. I've told you this already!" Joshua retorted, hearing Stephanie's cross reply.

Stephanie gulped, and then nodded. Joshua started towards the coffin that had appeared just a minute before.

Stephanie followed hesitantly at first, but then she ran towards Joshua, so that she was right beside him.

"Why, oh why, did I ever let you talk me into coming with you?" Stephanie complained.

"You decided of your own accord to come with me!" Joshua replied flatly.

"Yes, but you wanted me to come, didn't you?" Stephanie replied.


"Yup, I wanted you to come and you turned out to be pretty useful!" Joshua said amused.

"How?" Stephanie asked suspiciously.

"You found all the levers . . . by tripping over them!" Joshua said smiling.

"Very funny!" answered Stephanie sarcastically.

As soon as they reached the coffin, Stephanie said, "I refuse to open the coffin, that's your job!"

Joshua looked at Stephanie, exasperated and said, "Whatever!"

Stephanie looked at Joshua mischievously with her chin up.

Joshua muttered something under his breath, looking at Stephanie.

Joshua reached out his hand and touched the coffin. He leaned over and placed his hands so that he could open the lid. He tried to lift the coffin's lid, but to no avail.

He hesitated then said, "Stephanie, you need to help me to pick up this lid! It's impossible for one person to do alone!"

Stephanie was shaking her head before Joshua even finished his sentence.

"No, Joshua. I will not touch the coffin no matter what you say!" Stephanie complained.

Joshua sat down and said, "Then we can stay here until you give in and help me!"

Stephanie turned around to look at Joshua and froze. She stood rigidly, not moving a muscle.


Joshua, seeing Stephanie's expression looked at her questioningly and asked, "What?"

Stephanie did not move or answer. She seemed hypnotized.

"Stephanie, what is going on?" asked Joshua, starting to panic.

"I saw something move over there!" she hissed, pointing at a corner of the metallic room.

"It's probably just a rat or something!" Joshua whispered, trying to reassure himself as much as Stephanie.

"No, it wasn't! I'm sure it was a person!" Stephanie replied fiercely.

"How right you are!" screeched a voice.

"Joshua, tell me that was you!" Stephanie pleaded.

"It wasn't . . ." Joshua replied very quietly.

"He's right, it was not he!" cackled the voice.

Joshua felt his spine tingle and all his hair stand on end.

All of a sudden, someone stepped out of the shadows of the corner where Stephanie had pointed earlier.

Stephanie screamed in fear as Joshua scrambled out of the person's path.

The man had been going to tackle Joshua, but he moved out of the way just in time.

What was this person going to do to them? Would the person ruin Joshua and Stephanie's quest? Would the person try to hurt them?

# CHAPTER 16

## Marcelieuse Fonleiy

Joshua nearly choked as he caught the person's stench.

The man smelled of rot and death. He must have been in the pynazim for a long time.

Stephanie, blinded by her fear, kept screaming.

Joshua looked at the man that had run towards him.

He had long, black, scraggly hair that was encrusted with dirt. It was all tangled, and resembled a spider's web gone wrong.

Since the man wasn't wearing a shirt, Joshua could see that the man was very thin and pale.

Because Ringadore had four suns, the man should have been tanned.

Joshua realized that this was further proof that the man hadn't been outside for a long time.

The man ran towards Joshua and tackled him.

"What are you doing here?!" screamed the man.

"We're . . . searching . . . mummy!" Joshua gasped.

The man jumped up and looked at Joshua incredulously, and laughed. But as soon as he saw the lifted slab of wall and the coffin, he broke off very abruptly.

"You're serious!" the man exclaimed, wide-eyed.

"Absolutely serious!" Joshua shouted through Stephanie's consistent shrieks.

The man walked up to Stephanie and said, "If you don't shut your mouth, I will have to shut it for you and, trust me, that shall not be pleasant!"

Joshua gasped and looked at the man he had known for barely a minute shut Stephanie up.

Stephanie looked at the man, shocked and asked, "Who do you think you are?!"

"I am Marcelieuse Fonleiy. Who do you think you are?" the man retorted.

"My name is Stephanie. This is my friend Joshua and we are here to kill the mummy!" Stephanie answered icily.

Marcelieuse looked at the two children and said, "You will never accomplish that without my help."

"We don't want your help after what you said to me!" Stephanie replied adamantly.

"Yes, you will! I am the only one to know how to kill the mummy!" Marcelieuse replied, as adamantly as Stephanie.

"Stephanie, come here for a minute please!" Joshua said, interrupting Marcelieuse and Stephanie's quarrel.

Stephanie shot Marcelieuse one more menacing look and walked over to Joshua.

"What do you want?" she asked impatiently.

"I want to tell you that Marcelieuse Fonleiy might be helpful! Consider this; he is the only one to know how to kill the mummy!"

"Didn't you read the book? Doesn't it tell you how the guy killed the mummy?" Stephanie asked.

"Yes, I did read the book, but they don't exactly explain how to kill the mummy. You know it's not supposed to be an instruction manual!" Joshua responded.

"Oh, okay! But if he starts bossing us around, it's 'ciao' to him!" Stephanie gave in.

"Okay. I'll go tell Marcelieuse!" Joshua answered.

Joshua walked towards Marcelieuse Fonleiy.

He looked at him and said, "Stephanie and I have decided that you may accompany us on our quest."

Marcelieuse nodded his head and answered, "I was hoping you would say that."

"Yes. You may come along as long as you promise that you will help us kill the mummy. Will you keep that promise?" Joshua asked.

"I certainly will!" Marcelieuse retorted crossly.

Joshua led Marcelieuse over to Stephanie. They stood in silence for a moment, then Stephanie said, "I repeat that I will not touch the coffin."

"Oh that's okay," Joshua replied. "Marcelieuse will help me move the lid off the coffin. Won't you?"

Marcelieuse stared at Joshua for a moment, then answered, "Yes, I shall."


Joshua and Marcelieuse walked towards the coffin. Once again, Joshua placed his hands into the right position. Marcelieuse also placed his hands correctly. They both pulled with all of their strength, grunting with the effort.

Then, a crack was heard as Joshua and Marcelieuse tore the lid off of the coffin.

Stephanie watched them set the lid on the ground, and then joined them beside the open coffin.

Joshua looked into it. A bandaged hand immediately reached out and pulled Joshua into the coffin.

"Help!" Joshua shrieked, as he struggled to get out of the coffin.

"The mummy has made its first move! I must get light!" Marcelieuse screamed and ran away.

# CHAPTER 17

# The Fight

Joshua (who was currently in the coffin) was struggling and screaming.

He could feel the mummy's hand on his neck, choking him.

Joshua's screaming was cut short when the mummy started squeezing his neck even harder.

Joshua felt for sure that he was going to die when the hand on his neck disintegrated.

He took a look at the bottom of the coffin and saw a shining pile of ash.

Joshua wondered why the ashes were shining when he noticed that there was a huge hole in the top of the pynazim.

Stephanie's hand reached into the coffin and helped Joshua out.

"What happened?" asked Stephanie frantically, "Are you hurt? Where's the mummy?" asked Stephanie in mounting fear.

"Everything's fine!" answered Joshua reassuringly.

"But . . . But . . . the mummy?" Stephanie blubbered.

"I already told you—everything's fine! Where's Marcelieuse?" Joshua asked.

"Oh, he ran away when the mummy pulled you into the coffin," Stephanie answered.

"Why?" Joshua asked curiously.

"He said something about the mummy making its first move and having to make light," Stephanie answered in confusion, "Then that appeared," Stephanie said, pointing to the hole in the pynazim.

"I think that's what saved me!" Joshua exclaimed.

"So you're saying that this random hole in the ceiling destroyed the mummy?" Stephanie asked Joshua.

"Of course! The book said that the mummy disintegrated and that's exactly what it did. If Marcelieuse made that hole, he just saved my life!" Joshua revealed.

"So . . . Where's Marcelieuse?" Stephanie asked.

"I'm here!" replied Marcelieuse, puffing in exhaustion.

"So was it you that saved me?" asked Joshua.

"Yes, yes, yes . . ." Marcelieuse answered modestly, "I did say that I was the only one to know the secret to killing the mummy."

"Well, thank you!" Joshua exclaimed in gratitude.

"Oh, it was nothing!" Marcelieuse answered gruffly.

"So, now that the mummy's defeated, where's the portal?" Stephanie questioned Marcelieuse.

"Portal?" Marcelieuse asked in confusion.

"You know . . . a greenish pool that swirls around and around in circles," Stephanie explained.

"Oh yes . . . the green pools in the corner of the pynazim. I know what you are talking about," Marcelieuse replied.

"Would you please lead us to it?" Joshua asked hopefully.

"Yes, I will, if that is what you want," Marcelieuse answered.

No one moved or said anything for a minute, but then Stephanie broke the silence by saying, "Are we going or not?"

"Yes . . . off we go then!" Marcelieuse exclaimed and walked briskly out of the enclosed room and into the hallway.

Stephanie and Joshua followed him down the long corridors, trying to remember the way Marcelieuse was taking them, but to no avail.

There were too many twists and turns.

Marcelieuse turned left abruptly, almost leaving both Stephanie and Joshua behind.

They looked around the corner and saw an eerie green glow coming from the corridor that Marcelieuse had turned into.

Joshua followed Marcelieuse down the corridor and said, "Marcelieuse, I really want to thank you for saving my life and for all the help that you have given us on our quest."

"Think nothing of it," Marcelieuse answered pleasantly.

"Well, thank you anyways," Stephanie replied.

Joshua and Stephanie positioned themselves in front of the first portal and jumped.

As they were going through the portal, they could here the faint voice of Marcelieuse saying, "We shall see each other soon . . ."

# CHAPTER 18

## Back Home Once Again

Joshua and Stephanie landed on Joshua's bed.

Like the last adventure, no time had elapsed and no one had noticed that they had gone anywhere at all.

"That was some adventure!" Stephanie exclaimed.

"It sure was. I still have that mummy's finger marks on my neck!" Joshua answered, rubbing the back of his neck.

"That mummy was a jerk. It just came to life like that and it already has a grudge on you. The nerve of it!" Stephanie retorted.

Joshua rolled his eyes. He knew that Stephanie would have been the one pulled into the coffin if she was standing where he had been.

Stephanie kept complaining about the mummy when Joshua asked, "So when do you want to go on our next adventure?"

Stephanie stopped in mid-sentence and asked, "Are you joking? We've been back for a minute and you already want to go on our next adventure?"

"Of course I do. We may as well get this over with while we're here together. Tomorrow, I'll be busy and Monday, we won't be able to go anywhere except for school!" Joshua answered.

"It is a good point, but can't we wait until after lunch or something?" Stephanie pleaded.

"Well . . ." Joshua hesitated.

"Please!" Stephanie begged.

"Oh, okay!" Joshua finally answered.

"Yes!" Stephanie said, jumping off Joshua's bed and heading for the kitchen.

Joshua got up and took the book from where he'd left it.

He looked down the hallway towards his kitchen and remembered the long corridors in the pynazim.

His halls didn't look anything like the ones in the pynazim, but they still reminded him of his last adventure.

Joshua thought of what was about to come and followed Stephanie to the kitchen for lunch with the book under his arm.

When Joshua and Stephanie had finished lunch, they went back to Joshua's room and sat on Joshua's bed once again.

"Where are we going next?" Stephanie asked Joshua, eyeing the book on his lap quite suspiciously.

"We're going to the rain forest in Madagascar," Joshua answered Stephanie excitedly.

"Madagas-what?" Stephanie asked confused.

"Madagascar is an island to the right of Africa. We are going to a rainforest in the south of this island. The rainforest is now called the Manombo Tropical Rainforest," Joshua held his breath, hoping that Stephanie hadn't registered the word "now".

Stephanie's mouth was hanging open. She finally pulled herself together and said, "It's one thing that you know the name of this place, but you even know where it is!

"What happened to the old Joshua? Weren't you putting whoopee-cushions on Miss Caroline's chair just yesterday?" Stephanie blurted.

Joshua laughed and said, "People can change, can't they?"

Joshua thought about what he had just said and realized that he didn't feel the need to play stupid pranks on people anymore. The adventures had changed him.

Stephanie nodded, without saying anything.

"Well, shouldn't we be leaving?" Joshua asked Stephanie, wondering what she was thinking.

Stephanie nodded her head and said, "Yes, of course!"

Joshua opened the book. On the seventh and eight pages he saw their last adventure recorded. He looked at the ninth blank page and realized that this was his last adventure.

"On three," Joshua said, "One, Two, Three!"

They touched the blank page, closed their eyes, and were off into the unknown once again.

# CHAPTER 19

## The Manombo Forest

When Joshua and Stephanie opened their eyes, they found themselves under a canopy of thick green leaves.

The air was warm and humid, and there were all sorts of sounds that the two children had never heard before.

It was quite dark, since the canopy kept most of the sun out of the forest.

"Wow!" Stephanie exclaimed, lost for any other words.

"Uh-huh," Joshua agreed, "Did you know that there were eight species of lemurs in this forest?"

"No, I didn't," Stephanie answered, "I don't know much about this place. I didn't even know that Madagarshee existed!"

Joshua grinned, "Stephanie, it's called Madagascar!"

"I rest my case!" Stephanie said rolling her eyes.

Stephanie and Joshua laughed.

"So what are we supposed to do know?" Stephanie asked.

Joshua stopped laughing when he realised that he had to tell Stephanie a small detail about their trip,

"Stephanie, we're in year 1500." Maybe it wasn't such a small detail after all.

Stephanie looked daggers at Joshua and said, "You brought me to the sixteenth century and you didn't tell me?" she said, trying to keep her calm.

"I wouldn't put it that way but . . . I guess that's what I did," Joshua answered hesitantly.

"There *is* no other way to put it!" shrieked Stephanie, apparently having lost her calm.

Joshua flinched at Stephanie's shrill voice. Stephanie was really mad.

"I just can't believe that *you* did this to me!" she screamed, tearing at her hair.

She looked around her and ran into the forest.

"Wait!" Joshua cried, following her into the thick leaves and branches.

Just as he was breaking into a clearing he heard a scream. The scream had come from Stephanie. She was surrounded by thousands of bugs all covered with spikes.

"A little help here!" Stephanie screamed staring at the insects around her.

"Stephanie," Joshua said. "These are a type of grasshopper. In our time they are extinct, but in the 1500 they're still alive!"

"Thank you for the history lesson, but this really isn't the time!" Stephanie explained, flicking off one of the grasshoppers that had just hopped onto her.

"Keep them off, Steph. I'll think of something," Joshua said over Stephanie's snorts of disgust.

"What did the boy do?" Joshua asked himself . . . What did he do?

Then he remembered another important detail.

"Stephanie . . . Those grasshoppers are carnivores!" Joshua whispered, turning white.

# CHAPTER 20

## Carnivores!

"CARNIVORES!" Stephanie shrilled, turning red in the face.

Joshua nodded sheepishly, looking at the increasing number of grasshoppers trying to get onto Stephanie.

"They're carnivores and you forgot to tell me!" she shrieked, pulling grasshoppers out of her hair.

"Do you have a piece of meat on you?" Joshua inquired.

"*I* am the meat, Joshua!" Stephanie cried.

"Unfortunately I think you're right . . ." Joshua said nodding.

"Thanks for all the help!" Stephanie shot back. "Ow! They're biting, Josh, they're biting!"

Joshua was thinking when he heard a rustling in the forest behind him. Out came a dodo bird.

Joshua stared at it disbelievingly until he remembered that the dodos weren't yet extinct in the sixteenth century.

Joshua was going to help with their extinction . . .

He caught the dodo by the leg and threw it into the mass of grasshoppers.

The grasshoppers redirected their attention and jumped onto the dodo, biting into his flesh.

"Thank goodness that's passed!" Stephanie gasped, wiping her bleeding arms.

Joshua thanked himself, knowing that Stephanie wouldn't bother saying anything after he had almost gotten her killed.

Stephanie didn't say a word for some time, but followed Joshua when he walked into the forest away from the clearing.

"Sorry," Joshua said when Stephanie finally caught up with him. "I didn't mean to drag you into something you didn't want anything to do with."

"It's fine . . ." Stephanie said looking at Joshua.

"So I guess it's time to go find the portal!" Stephanie said changing her mood quite dramatically.

Joshua flinched and said, "We're not done here yet."

"Awww!" Stephanie cried, not happy with the news.

"First, we have to find someone to show us the location of the portal," Joshua explained.

"Why? Why do we have to be the only two kids in the world to have to deal with giants and mushroom creatures and evil geniuses and carnivorous grasshoppers? Why? I want to go home!" Stephanie exclaimed.

"So do I, Stephanie, but this is the last story in the book and we have to finish our adventures," Joshua replied instantly.

"Then let's get this over with! What happened in the book? Where did the boy go? Where's the portal?" Stephanie asked impatiently.

"I don't remember well, but I think that he . . ." Joshua was interrupted by Stephanie before he finished his sentence.

"You're the one that read the book! You should know what happened!" Stephanie screamed so loudly that the birds in the trees above flew away, squawking in alarm.

"Stephanie. I told you before that these adventures would have a meaning and that I am sure they will lead us to something. I think our answers will be revealed in this adventure," Joshua explained.

Stephanie looked at Joshua questioningly and said, "You never told me that."

Joshua opened his mouth, but he was speechless.

Here he was in the middle of a jungle in Madagascar in the sixteenth century; his last adventure and he had forgotten to tell Stephanie another important detail.

Their adventures would have a meaning, but he hadn't told anyone what he thought.

Joshua sighed deeply and started, "Ever since I opened the book, I knew there was something special about it. When I got sucked into it for the first time, I felt for sure that I'd find out why in the last adventure.

"If we finish this adventure, I will feel that my mission has been accomplished."

Stephanie nodded slowly, comprehending all the information Joshua had thrown at her so abruptly.

Finally she said, "Ok . . . So where do we have to go?"

Joshua smiled and said, "From what I remember, the boy wandered around until he'd found a hut."

"A hut," Stephanie exclaimed, "there could be a hut anywhere in this humongous jungle. We'll be wandering for the rest of our lives, if you can't remember exactly where the hut was."

Joshua nodded, deep in thought, "The boy found a hut. There was a troll inside the hut who tried to kill him."

"Whoa! You never told me there was something else that was going to try to kill me!" Stephanie cried.

"There's no backing out now, Steph. We have to find the troll, the hut and the portal, if we are to get back home," Joshua reasonably explained.

"I guess . . ." Stephanie murmured hesitantly.

"That's it!" Joshua cried, making Stephanie jump in surprise.

"What's it?" Stephanie asked.

"The boy followed a wise old tortoise to the troll's hut," Joshua exclaimed.

"A wise old tortoise! What kind of a fairytale is that? And anyways, there are probably thousands of tortoises in this jungle. How would we know which one is which?" Stephanie asked frantically.

Joshua nodded his head hopelessly, "I knew that you'd say that!"

Seeing Joshua's saddened expression, Stephanie sighed and muttered, "I guess we can go on. Let's find that tortoise."

Joshua beamed and walked purposefully into the forest, "This way. I remember now. The boy went straight into the forest and found the tortoise right . . ."

"Wow!" Stephanie cried pointing at a huge lump on the ground. There was the tortoise, just lying there, waiting.

"I see you have found me once again," the tortoise croaked.

"What do you mean, 'again'?" Joshua asked, intrigued by the size of their companion.

"You found me a thousand years ago when the book was written and you have found me once again," continued the tortoise, "You are the descendant of the boy that found me that long, long time ago."

Joshua's eyes widened and he said, "The book is really that old?"

"Yes, it is. My name is Galileo and I am the guardian of the book you now have in your possession," Galileo explained briefly.

Stephanie stood there, looking on in amazement. She, who had come into this adventure by fluke, was standing in front of the oldest living thing on earth.

"I am the descendant of the boy?" Joshua asked, open mouthed.

"Yes, you are. You have to finish this adventure to accomplish the boy's mission. He never accomplished his, but was killed by the troll," Galileo said.

"But the book says that the boy makes it!" Joshua exclaimed.

"The book is lying. I wrote that ending for the story in hope that one day, someone would discover the purpose of the blank pages and come and complete what your ancestor could not," Galileo explained.

"But how? I'm only a boy!" Joshua exclaimed.

"Yes, but look how far you have gotten. This is the last adventure in the book. You cannot turn back now."

Stephanie, feeling ignored asked, "So, what's my part in this?"

Galileo turned to Stephanie, leaving Joshua staring into space.

"You, Stephanie, will have to help Joshua finish his adventure. There will come a time when he makes a mistake and you will have to help him get through that hard time," Galileo explained.

Stephanie looked at Joshua, turned back to Galileo and asked, "What if I can't help him though?"

"You will know what is right and what you will have to do," Galileo answered, ending their conversation.

"Now, be off and let your feet guide you on your way," Galileo stated, turning around and walking back into the forest.

Joshua sat and sighed, "He didn't really tell us anything important."

"Of course he did. Didn't you hear him? He told you that you were the boy's descendant! It proves you're right! There is a purpose to our adventures!" Stephanie shouted wildly.

"Okay, but where do we go? He didn't tell us anything about that, did he?" Joshua asked.

"Yes, he did! He told us to let our feet guide us on our way! What's up with you, Josh?" Stephanie exclaimed.

"That's not much to rely on," Joshua said. "It's like telling us to let ourselves get hit by a car and that nothing will happen."

"Well, if you won't come, I'll go find that portal on my own!" Stephanie cried, storming into the forest.

Joshua sighed again, got up and followed Stephanie.

Stephanie saw Joshua following her, but didn't stop. She kept going, "letting her feet guide her".

Joshua knew that Stephanie had seen him, and kept going after her. He knew that Stephanie was going the right way.

Stephanie kept walking, looking back at Joshua, when she bumped into something.

Joshua smiled. She had found the hut.

# CHAPTER 21

## The Hut

Stephanie stopped and rubbed her head. There was a hut, blending in with the forest, looking as if it belonged.

"Huh?" Stephanie exclaimed, confused.

Joshua ran up behind her, laughing and patting her on the back, "You found the troll's hut!"

Stephanie nodded, wide-eyed at her discovery.

Joshua walked around the wooden building, looking for a door. Stephanie followed close behind.

Joshua stopped in mid-step and Stephanie bumped into him. A door had opened right in front of them, and Joshua had frozen in fear.

Out of the door came an ugly troll.

The troll wore red stockings up to his knees, accompanied by a pair of ripped, dirty, cut-off jeans.

He wore a small brown rag as a shirt and his eyes were so tiny that it seemed impossible for him to see.

His face was wrinkled and brown, he had a very small amount of hair on his head and his triangular ears stuck straight up from his head.

Stephanie turned and ran away, calling Joshua, "Run, Joshua! Run!"

He stood there, staring at the creature in pure terror.

Joshua had seen many other uglier, bigger, and more horrible creatures than this one, but he was still petrified by it.

Stephanie ran back and took Joshua by the arm and pulled. Joshua didn't move an inch. He really was petrified!

"Run, Stephanie . . . Go without me righ—," Joshua started, but the troll put his hand over Joshua's mouth.

Stephanie stood there, staring at the troll taking Joshua into the hut.

Galileo had been right! Joshua had made a mistake by looking for an entry into the hut. Now *she* had to rescue *him*.

Meanwhile, the troll let go of Joshua's mouth and sat him roughly in a chair, tying his arms behind his back.

The inside of the hut smelled of decay like the ogres' cave. It was a huge mess and nothing looked as if it had ever had a place.

The couches were worn and full of moss and the walls looked like they would collapse at any given moment.

In the middle of the room was a rickety staircase leading down into the basement.

The light that filtered through the cracked windows was pale and didn't make much of a difference in the room.

"Let me go!" Joshua shouted at the troll's ugly face.

"Me no want to. Me want you to be with me forever and ever as servant you be!" the troll explained in his strange accent.

"I don't!" Joshua shouted.

"Me do!" the troll answered back.

"You won't!" Stephanie shrieked, crashing through one of the windows.

"How you get here! Me no want you here!" the troll screamed at Stephanie.

Stephanie jumped up from where she had landed and banged the troll on the head with a very thick and heavy branch.

The troll fell to the ground and screamed in pain.

Joshua looked on in amazement. Stephanie had possibly saved him.

Stephanie hit the troll again and this time he fell still. He was finally unconscious.

Stephanie got up, wiped her hands in satisfaction and walked over to where Joshua was sitting.

She bent down on one knee and untied the complicated knot the troll had tied.

"Thank you!" Joshua said, rubbing his wrists where the rope had left a mark on his skin.

"Come on. Let's go down the stairs," Stephanie said, pulling Joshua by the arm.

Joshua followed, looking down at the troll as he passed by.

Joshua and Stephanie ran down the stairs, careful not to walk on the many rotten steps.

The basement was even worse than the top floor.

The ground here was made out of packed dirt. The walls looked even more unsteady than upstairs and the air here smelled so bad that Joshua tried not to breathe it in.

The light here though, was surprisingly better than upstairs.

Stephanie wondered why and looked in one of the corners of the room. There, in that little corner were six little pools of water. They were round and glowed like the moon. They were the portals.

"Joshua! The portals!" Stephanie exclaimed, running towards the closest one.

Joshua nodded and followed Stephanie but was tripped by something. He tried to get up but was held down by a powerful force.

The troll had awoken and there he was, lying on Joshua keeping him on the ground.

"Stephanie, help!" Joshua screamed, punching the troll's nose.

"You no get away from me! Oh, no, you will not! Me want to keep you, and this time, me eat you!" the troll bellowed, and punched Joshua back.

Stephanie turned and ran towards the troll. She kicked his head and he jumped off of Joshua yelling in agony. Stephanie kicked his shins and he fell to the ground, whimpering.

Joshua jumped up and ran towards the corner, Stephanie close behind.

The troll attempted to get up, but fell back to the ground again, "Me no want you go away!"

Stephanie stopped in front of the portal, gave one last look at the troll and jumped into the portal with Joshua.

# CHAPTER 22

## The Meeting

Joshua landed on his bed with a big thump. Stephanie followed, making the same amount of noise.

Joshua's mom walked into the room and exclaimed, "Joshua! You're bleeding! What happened?"

Joshua grinned, wiping the blood away from his nose and said, "You wouldn't believe me if I told you!"

"You guys didn't have a fight, did you?" Joshua's mom asked, concerned.

Stephanie and Joshua looked at each other and laughed. This was so far away from the truth.

Joshua's mom eyed them suspiciously and walked away saying, "I'll fetch some paper towel."

As soon as she came back and gave Joshua the paper towel to wipe his nose, Joshua closed the door and went to his shelf to get the book.

He delicately placed it on his bed and just as he was about to open it, Stephanie grabbed his arm and said, "Look, Joshua! They're all here!"

"Who's here? What are you talking about?" Joshua exclaimed, looking at Stephanie.

"Look in your room! They're all here!" she persisted.

Joshua looked and what he saw was extraordinary. His room had changed into a vast valley full of lush green grass. On the grass were standing all of his friends from the book.

Alexis was there, looking as beautiful as when he had met her. The dragon was right there by her side, accompanied by all his children.

On the other side were some of his other friends, including the brownies (Christopher standing, looking at Joshua very proudly) and Henry and his master.

In the middle of the valley stood Marcelieuse Fonleiy, a little mass of flesh-eating grasshoppers and his friend, Galileo.

Galileo walked up to Joshua, followed by Alexis, Christopher, Marcelieuse and Henry.

"You have done well, child," Galileo started. "Your friend and you have accomplished your mission and are now heroes."

"We never wanted to be heroes though!" Joshua said respectfully.

"You are to us though, my children!" Alexis proclaimed, looking at both children lovingly.

Stephanie's eyes were wide and she was staring at Alexis in pure wonder, "You're beautiful!"

The unicorn laughed and bent her head to Stephanie in respect.

Stephanie smiled and turned to Joshua, who was still talking with his friends.

"Did you see that, Joshua? She bowed!" Stephanie asked.

"I did," Joshua said and continued on speaking with his friends.

"Now read the last page!" Christopher said and disappeared along with all of their other friends.

Stephanie said, "Where did they go?"

"They're gone . . . forever," Joshua answered, very disappointed.

"How do you know?" Stephanie asked.

"Galileo told me," Joshua answered briefly.

"Oh . . ." Stephanie said, her hopeful look vanishing.

They stood in silence for a minute. Stephanie sighed and said, "Find the book. Christopher wants us to look at the last page."

Joshua walked over to the book, picked it up and flipped to the last page.

On it was written their latest adventure accompanied by two simple words:

The End . . .

To be continued . . .